The Venom in the Valentine

Valentine

Viola Roberts Cozy Mystery

Book 5

Shéa MacLeod

DEDICATION

To YK

Because you are fabulous. Like purple glitter.

Chapter 1

"Now that's what I call stunning." My best friend, Cheryl Delaney, dropped her bags in the middle of the hotel room and stared out the large picture window.

Beyond the glass pane, the ocean heaved itself up onto the dark rocks edging the beach, sending white plumes high into the air. Dark clouds scudded along in the sky above, while pines tossed wildly in the wind below. February along the Oregon Coast tended toward the wild side.

"I still can't believe Lucas ditched you, Viola." Cheryl didn't turn around, her gaze still on the surging surf below. "And on Valentine's, too. Such a shame. Still, his loss is my gain!"

I scowled. "Lucas didn't ditch me. His flight was delayed. He'll be here on the day."

Like me, my boyfriend, Lucas Salvatore, was a writer. In fact, we'd met at a writer's conference in Florida and the rest, as they say, was history. Unlike me, he was the sort of writer whose novels got made into movies, so he was in demand as a speaker at conferences all over the world. Unfortunately, a snowstorm on the East Coast had grounded flights and left him stranded three thousand miles from home just a few short days before the Big V: Valentine's Day. It was supposed to be our first as a couple. We'd planned to spend it at The Grand Seaview Resort, one of Oregon's most romantic ocean side hotels. Instead of canceling, Lucas insisted Cheryl take his place. Hopefully he'd be able to join later. I wasn't holding my breath.

"This actually works out great for me," I said, setting my own suitcase carefully on the rack provided.

"Really? How's that?"

"Well." I unzipped my case and began carefully unpacking. I was a nester, and hated living out of a suitcase. I didn't feel at home until my shirts were in the top drawer and my pants in the bottom. You know how it is. "I've got proofs due on my latest novel, *The Rancher's Ransomed Bride*. This way I don't have to feel guilty about working on it over Valentine's."

This time Cheryl did turn. "Viola Roberts!" She propped her hands on her hips and glared at me. "We're here to relax, not work."

I hid a smirk. An angry Cheryl was a bit like an enraged pixie: adorable and hard to take seriously. Her short, spiky dark hair only added to the image. She was a smidge shorter than my own five foot five and delicately slender where I was voluptuous and curvy. Cheryl was also a writer, though her forte was mysteries and thrillers where mine was historical romances of the Old West variety. Which meant lots of ranchers and cowboys and mail order brides.

Cheryl and I had met shortly after I moved to Astoria, Oregon and joined the local writers' group.

We'd hit it off immediately. And, although we'd both left the original group, we'd remained fast friends.

"I know we're here to relax, and I will, but I've got to finish the proofs first. They're due on V-Day."

She scowled, a line forming between her brows. "You should tell your editor to hold her britches. This is a holiday."

"I'll get right on that." Since my publisher was me, I had no intention of listening. Deadlines were deadlines. Otherwise I'd never get anything done. Besides, I was so used to spending Valentine's Day alone, the idea that I actually had someone to celebrate with this year was…unnerving.

"Fine," she said sulkily. "Let's go get a drink at the bar, at least. Then you can get to your precious proofs."

"Thank you." Part of me itched to get started, but another part of me could really use that drink. Driving down the coast from Astoria had been a little harrowing, thanks to the wind. More than once I'd imagined us plummeting—car and all—over the edge of Highway 101 and into the sea. I have way too much imagination for my own good.

Our suite was one of the very best, on the top floor, so we took the elevator to the lobby. The large area was dotted with clusters of sofas and comfy chairs. The open space was meant for guests to sit and relax while enjoying the view from the floor to ceiling windows spanning the entire front of the building. Few were interested at the view as the panes were splatted with drops of moisture, and the sky loomed dark and ominous.

"Looks like a storm," Cheryl said. "Let's sit near the fire."

"Sure."

Off in one corner was a massive fireplace of local river stone. A real wood fire radiated tremendous amounts of heat. Cheryl didn't seem to mind, but I, on the other hand, immediately broke out in a sweat. I moved my chair a little ways back to avoid the worst of the heat.

In another corner was a small bar serving bottles of beer and glasses of wine. No hard liquor or mixed cocktails. Which was a shame as I fancied my favorite: blackberry bourbon. Instead I ordered a rich Malbec while Cheryl chose a lighter Pinot. I had to admit, relaxing with a glass of wine in front of a roaring fire while a storm raged outside was just what the doctor ordered. I was half tempted to forget those proofs.

"Are these seats taken?"

I glanced up to find a middle aged man and someone I assumed was his wife. He was dressed in neatly pressed khaki's and a blue button-down shirt. He looked like the briefcase carrying kind. Lawyer, maybe.

"Not at all. Have a seat." I waved magnanimously.

"I'm Lawrence Tupper—you can call me Larry— and this is my wife, Angie. We're here to celebrate our twenty-sixth wedding anniversary." He gave me a wide smile. He was an attractive man, for his age, with pure, white hair and sparkling blue eyes. He had only a small paunch around the middle.

"Congratulations!" Cheryl beamed happily and raised her glass in a toast.

"Thank you," Angie said. Her hair was dark and sleek—bottle, no doubt—and her age carefully hidden beneath a thick layer of makeup. From the tautness around her eyes and throat, I was guessing there'd been a face lift or two involved. Her smile seemed fake, never reaching her eyes, and I wondered if she really wanted to be here. "How long have you been together?" she asked.

I stared at her, confused for a moment. "Oh, we're not a couple. We're best friends. For over three years now."

"I apologize. I just assumed... You know, with it being Valentine's Day and all." Angie looked away, clearly embarrassed.

"Don't worry about it," I said with a wave of my hand. The wine was sending a warm glow through me and I was feeling relaxed and happy. "We know each other so well, it's an easy mistake." It was kind of funny though, since Cheryl could be downright boy crazy. When she wasn't on one of her dating moratoriums. She didn't have the best luck when it came to men.

"It's nice that you can celebrate your wedding anniversary here," Cheryl said. "It seems like such a romantic hotel."

"Very," Larry said. "That's why I chose it. Though it is a bit out of the way."

He wasn't kidding about that. The fifty year-old luxury resort had been built about half-way between two towns—Lincoln City and Newport—smack dab on the ocean in the middle of nowhere. You had to drive down a narrow, winding drive to get to it. It had its own restaurant, spa, and work-out room as well as a small golf course. There was no reason to leave the resort unless you wanted to, and during the stormy season—which was now—it could become quite isolated.

"It's perfect for a romantic getaway," Cheryl assured him.

"Did anyone ever tell you that you look just like Halle Berry?" Larry asked.

"No, never," Cheryl lied politely. She only got that line from just about everyone she met. "How sweet of you."

"She looks nothing like Halle Berry," Angie said tartly.

There was a flash of something in her eyes. Jealousy, perhaps? Her reaction was odd, because Larry hadn't been flirting with Cheryl. He'd just been complimentary. The entire time he'd held his wife's hand as if he couldn't bear to let her go. Was she just insecure? Or was there something deeper going on?

Perhaps you're right," Larry said soothingly. "Oh, look. Our reservations are in an hour. We should get ready. Ladies, if you'll excuse us?"

We murmured our goodbyes. Angie didn't even look our way. Definitely something odd with that woman.

I reminded myself firmly that I was there to relax and finish my proofs. Not get all up in someone else's business. Still, Angie Tupper's reaction remained with me the rest of the evening.

Shéa MacLeod

Chapter 2

Cheryl and I lingered over our wine until after dark, then decided on an early dinner. Lunch had been less than stellar. Normally I like to stop at one of those little mom and pop diners that pepper the coast, but my favorite one had been closed, so we'd chosen a cafe on the outskirts of Lincoln City. The sandwiches had been barely edible and the soup lukewarm and a suspicious shade of green. By five, my stomach was already growling loud enough to wake the dead.

The hotel dining room was a comfortable blend of cozy rustic and elegant modern. After a delicious meal of steak, delicious apple pie for dessert, and more wine, Cheryl and I staggered back to our room.

"What they need is a wheelbarrow service," Cheryl said. "I am so full!"

"No kidding." I flopped on my bed and stared at the ceiling, willing myself to digest faster. Proofs would have to wait until tomorrow.

"What's this?" Cheryl bent down and picked up a white envelope off the floor. She frowned at it. "There's no name. Just our room number."

"Open it. Maybe it's some kind of welcome from the hotel or something. We're in a suite, after all." I would have preferred a fruit basket. Or, better yet, chocolates.

She pried open the flap and pulled out a folded sheet of paper. "Oh, my."

"What?"

"Read this." She handed me what appeared to be a handwritten note on the hotel's stationary.

I sat up and focused on the spidery letters. "Go home, lesbians. No one wants your type here. Get out before it's too late." I snorted. "Someone's idea of a joke."

"It's a warning," Cheryl said solemnly.

I rolled my eyes. "Please. As if being a lesbian is the worst thing ever. This is Oregon. Not some backwater. Even if we were lesbians, no one would care."

Cheryl sunk into the window seat. "This may be Oregon, but there are people here from other places. Like the Tuppers? That Angie thought we were a couple. Maybe she wrote it."

"She'd have had to have written it before they came downstairs for drinks. And they hadn't even met us yet."

"She could have written it after."

"But she knew by then that we're not a couple," I pointed out.

"Maybe she didn't believe us."

"Frankly, I don't care who wrote it. It's stupid. I'm

not giving it another thought." And with that I crumpled up the letter and threw it in the garbage.

#

The next morning, I threw back the curtains to find the sky such a hard, bright blue, my eyes hurt to look at it. The ocean had calmed, the green-blue waves only sending the occasional spray skyward. The storm had passed and it looked more like summer than winter.

Cheryl grumbled something unintellible and rolled over, pulling the bedspread over her head. I grinned. Cheryl was usually the morning person. I was the one who slept until well after nine and needed multiple cups of coffee to recover. But this morning I was wide awake and ready to go.

After pulling on sweat pants and a hoodie, I tucked my laptop under one arm and headed downstairs to breakfast. Not exactly glamorous, but I worked better in pajamas, and sweats were the closest thing to pajamas acceptable for public wear. Besides, I had no one to impress. All thoughts of dressing up went out the window when my romantic assignation turned into a BFF getaway.

The dining room had the same wall-to-wall windows as the lobby. The vista was stunning as the morning light danced on the waves like living diamonds. I chose the same table Cheryl and I had the night before and plunked down where I could easily see the view. As I set up my laptop, the waitress—a young twenty-something with a blonde pony-tail and a nose piercing partially hidden under a beige band aid—brought me coffee and took my breakfast order: Eggs benedict with hash browns.

I found the upscale rustic ambiance and the solitude soothing. The dining room was mostly empty. I wasn't sure if that was because the hotel was mostly empty, or if other guests were enjoying breakfast in bed. In either case, I had my own little corner to myself. I was deep in the proofs when a voice startled me back to reality.

"Oh, Viola, you've got the best view in the house. Mind if we join you?"

I blinked up at Larry Tupper as my brain readjusted to the real world. "Um."

"She's busy, Larry." Angie's tone was annoyed. I was betting she had planned a private breakfast with her husband, not another group get-to-know-you with me.

Some mean little part of me took an immediate dislike to Angie Tupper. I gave them both a beaming smile. "Oh, no worries. I need a break. Sit." I gestured expansively at the table.

They took   seats and the waitress took orders. "Lovely day, isn't it?" Larry said, gazing out the window with a pleased smile, as if he'd arranged for the weather himself. "They say it'll get up to sixty-five today. Not really what I expected in February."

"We have those odd quirks of weather once in a while," I explained. "I remember one year it hit low seventies around Valentine's Day. We were all running around in shorts." I wasn't about to admit that I'd been a teenager and it had been nearly thirty years since that day.

Larry barked out a laugh. Angie made a sour face, her unnaturally plump lips puckering. In the harsh winter light, she looked much older than she had last night.

"We've certainly been enjoying our stay despite the weather. Haven't we, darling?" Larry asked.

Angie sipped her black coffee—the only thing she'd ordered—and gave a shrug of one bare shoulder. Despite the fact it was middle of winter, she was wearing a sleeveless top and thin, linen trousers as if we were in Hawaii, not Oregon.

"When did you arrive?" I asked.

"Day before yesterday. And it's been fantastic. Perhaps now that the weather has turned nice, we can explore one of the nearby towns. I hear there's an excellent book store in Depot Bay." He looked at his wife, clearly eager for the adventure, but Angie kept her eyes glued to the scenery, a look of abject boredom on her face.

"Sounds like a great plan. Too bad I'm stuck here with work or I'd tag along." Not that I had any intention of doing such a thing, but it made Angie squirm.

Larry gave me a sympathetic smile. "What a shame. But at least this is a nice spot for it."

"Viola," Cheryl appeared from behind a potted plant, her hair rumpled and eyes sleepy, "what'd you do with that letter?. I told the manager about it and she wants to keep it for evidence." "I threw it away. It was a bad joke. Nothing more."

Cheryl crossed her arms. "She wants to see it."

"What's this about a letter?" Larry asked.

I explained about the note. "It's clearly someone being a jerk. It's ridiculous."

"Sounds like a poisoned pen letter," Larry said. "Very popular in detective fiction."

"He's right," Cheryl said. "Agatha Christie used it in *The Moving Finger*."

Angie made a moue of distaste, but said nothing. She took a delicate sip of her black coffee then pulled out a paperback which she promptly began reading. I noticed vaguely it was one of Lucas's older titles. I didn't bother to mention it.

"That's fiction," I pointed out. "In real life people don't send letters like that anymore."

"I wouldn't be so hasty to dismiss it," Larry advised.

"I'm with Larry," Cheryl said stubbornly. "And so is the manager. She says we're not the only ones who've gotten nasty notes."

That caught my interest. It caught Larry's, too. "Really?" he asked. "Who else has gotten one?"

Cheryl sank into the empty seat at the table. The waitress rushed over to fill a coffee cup for her. "Thanks." She turned back to us. "Somebody named Miriam Bartolomey. She's from South America or something."

"What did her note say?" I asked.

"Apparently, the writer accused her of being a terrorist. Which is ridiculous. The woman is eighty." Cheryl dumped cream and sugar in her cup, chugged down her coffee, and looked around for the waitress. "Poor woman. All she wants is a vacation and she gets hate mail."

"Is she the only one?" Larry asked.

"Far as I know," Cheryl said. "But now that two rooms have gotten them, I bet there'll be more."

She had a point. Poison pen letters tended to come in multiples. Besides, proofing was giving me a headache. I needed a break and curiosity was getting the better of me.

"I'd like to talk to Miriam Bartolomey," I said. "Before the next letter drops."

Cheryl gave me a wicked smile. "You're in luck. She's hanging out in the hot tub."

Chapter 3

Steam curled in tendrils toward the ceiling, the thick vapor turning the air thick as pea soup. Chlorine stung my nose and made my eyes water. I tightened the belt of my plush, terry cloth robe provided by the hotel and waded in. Figuratively speaking.

I hate swimsuits. Not because I'm ashamed of my body, though the American fashion police would love to make me believe my body wasn't good enough. It's that swimsuits are, frankly, hideous and ill-fitting. Even a lot of thin women look far from attractive in swimsuits. It's as if the designers go out of their way to emphasize every lump, bump, and bit of pale, wobbly flesh.

Cheryl followed me in and quickly dropped her robe. She, naturally, looked amazing in a simple pale blue one-piece. She sank into the hot water with a blissed out sigh. "This feels amazing. Come on, Viola."

I dropped my own robe on a nearby chair and climbed in. She was right. It did feeling amazing. But we weren't here to relax. We had a job to do.

The only other person in the tub was a woman so old even her wrinkles had wrinkles. She looked like a leather handbag that had seen better days. Even in the hot tub she wore a smear of magenta lipstick that bled into the wrinkles around her mouth. She gave us a toothy grin and I realized the lipstick also decorated her teeth. I made a mental note to make a pact with Cheryl that we'd never allow lipstick to decorate our teeth no matter how old we got.

"Are you Miriam Bartolemy?" Cheryl asked bluntly.

I elbowed her. I had been planning to go for subtle. Well, semi-subtle, anyway.

"I am. And you are?" Miriam Bartolomey had a thick accent from somewhere very far south of the border.

"I'm Viola," I said. "And this is Cheryl."

"The manager gave us your name," Cheryl said.

Miriam's eyes widened, her sparse, gray eyebrows rising toward iron-gray hair piled artfully on top her head. "Really? How interesting. Why would she do that?"

"She said you got a poisoned pen letter," I said.

Miriam frowned, the lipstick streaks appeared to spread even further across her face. "A what kind of letter? I'm sorry. English is not my first language."

"A mean letter. Unsigned," I supplied. "Maybe accusing you of something or threatening you."

"Oh, that." Miriam shrugged one boney shoulder. "It was nothing. Some silly, childish game."

"Your English is very good," Cheryl said. "Where are you from?"

"Paraguay, though I've lived in Los Angeles for many years now. I was a dancer, once upon a time.

Even did a movie with Debbie Reynolds." She threw back her shoulders proudly and gave a little shimmy.

"I bet you did, you saucy minx." I winked and Miriam laughed.

"That's so cool." Cheryl beamed with excitement. "I love Debbie Reynolds."

"Do you remember what the note said?" I asked.

"Of course. It said I was a terrorist and if I did not leave immediately and return to my country, the writer would tell the authorities. It is all nonsense, of course. I am eighty-five years old at a spa in the middle of nowhere. What do they think I'm gonna do?" She cackled as if it were the funniest thing ever. I wasn't sure I'd be so calm if someone accused me of being a terrorist.

We stayed in the hot tub awhile longer. Mostly because it felt good, but also because Cheryl was enamored of Miriam's stories about working with the late Debbie Reynolds. I wondered if they were true, or if they were the ramblings of a bored old woman who wanted to seem more interesting than she was. Whatever the case, she was definitely not a terrorist. Any more than Cheryl and I were lesbian lovers. The poison pen writer was way off the mark. So, why send such ridiculous letters? Did he, or she, honestly think what they were writing was true? Or did they not care and simply want to stir the pot?

I finally made my excuses and exited the steamy room, leaving Cheryl to chat with Miriam. The lobby was downright chilly after the heat of the hot tub. I stopped at the front desk, ignoring the water I was dripping all over the stone floor.

There was only one person behind the desk. He was close to my age—early to mid-forties—with thinning mousy hair and excellent posture. Silver rimmed reading glasses perched on the end of his slender nose as he peered at the computer screen. He glanced up. "May I help you?"

I glanced at his nametag. "Hi, Jeremiah. Have you heard about the poison pen letters going around?"

He slipped off his glasses. "I have. Horrible, isn't it? Although ridiculous. I mean, that ancient woman a terrorist? Insane."

"And you heard about the one my friend and I got? We're in room 405."

"Oh yes. Why anyone would think that an insult..." he shook his head. "This is the twenty-first century."

"Indeed. Has anyone else received letters?" I asked.

"Not that I'm aware of, however my manager just stepped out and will be back in an hour or so. Perhaps you can speak to her? After you change." He glanced pointedly at the pool of water spreading from beneath me.

"I'll do that." My flip flops squelched against the tile as I strode toward the elevator. The doors slid open to reveal Larry Tupper.

"Viola! You'll never guess what happened." He thrust a sheet of paper at me.

I took it, and saw scrawled in black letters, "I know you are going to kill your wife." I stared at Larry. "You got one, too."

"Yeah. It's insane, of course." He yanked the paper out of my hands and crumpled it into a ball. "I love my wife. I would never harm her. This lunatic needs to be stopped." His cheeks were pink and his eyes snapped with genuine anger.

"I agree. And you need to keep that note."

He frowned. "Why?"

"Evidence. So far the poison pen writer has delivered three letters. And it looks like each one is getting nastier. I'm going to talk to the hotel manager in a bit, but it might be time to bring in the police."

He looked like he might refuse, but then handed over the note. "Would you give it to them? I need to get back to Angie. She's extremely upset." The doors slid shut in my face. Dammit. I'd have to wait for the elevator to return.

I found it hard to imagine Angie the Ice Queen being effected by anything as stupid as an anonymous letter, but who knew. People were funny. Maybe it had hit her wrong. Or maybe... I remembered Angie's coldness from the night before. For all their hand-holding coupleness, it had seemed forced. Faked. At least on Angie's part. It had felt to me like Larry was genuinely in love with his wife. But maybe I was wrong. Maybe their relationship was on the rocks. Maybe Larry really had considered killing her.

I shook my head. "Don't be ridiculous. You're seeing murder everywhere."

"Excuse me?"

I glanced over to see a slender, ferret faced woman staring at me. Her slightly protruding eyes were wide and horrified. She clutched a poppy red bag to her chest as if to protect herself from the crazy woman.

"Uh, nothing. Talking to myself. I'm a writer."

"Oh." But she scurried off as if I might pull out a chainsaw at any moment.

I laughed softly to myself as I stepped onto the elevator to be whisked to the top floor. With a soft plink noise, the keycard unlocked the door to the suite, and something crinkled beneath my flip flop as I stepped into the room. I leaned down and picked up an envelope. Another poison pen letter perhaps? Except the envelope was red, not white. A Valentine then.

I ripped it open and pulled out a heart shaped card. Inside it read, "Leave or die."

# # #

The manager was a surprisingly young woman—perhaps early thirties—with carroty red hair and freckles on every inch of exposed skin. She gave me a sunny smile as Jeremiah, the guy at the front desk, ushered me into her office.

It was a very plain, basic sort of room. A single window looked out onto the parking lot. The desk was laminated particle board. The super cheap kind that probably came from some bulk warehouse somewhere. A sad plastic plant sat on top of a metal filing cabinet. For such an expensive place, I would have expected a nicer office for the manager.

"Anna Kettrick. Day manager. How may I help you?" She shook my hand firmly, but her hands were a little too cool, like she had bad circulation.

"Viola Roberts, guest. I want to talk to you about these poison pen letters."

"Please sit down." She waved me to a hard, molded plastic chair. "I'm sure it's just a silly prank." Her cheeks pinked a little.

"You mean you hope it is. It's pretty nasty for a silly prank. People are really upset." Well, Larry Tupper had been. Like me, Miriam had brushed hers off. "In fact, I received two letters and this last one was a threat." I handed her the letter.

She glanced at it, jaw working. "Ghastly."

"I think we should call the police."

"There's no need for that." Anna gripped the edge of her desk. "I will look into this myself. I'm certain it's a prank and the culprit will soon be found and dealt with accordingly."

I gazed at her. "Why are you reluctant to bring in the police?"

"Listen, I'm new here. And the last thing I need is to get a reputation for having the police out to the hotel. Surely this can be dealt with quietly."

I thought it over. I understood her concern. They were just letters, after all. Nothing bad had happened. "Fine. But if any more guests get letters, I'm going to call the police myself."

Chapter 4

The rest of the day passed quickly. I finished the proofs on *The Rancher's Ransomed Bride* and sent it off to the formatter. Cheryl and I got a couples massage. I'd have enjoyed it more with Lucas, but it was still fun. Afterward we had mani pedis. Cheryl chose bubble gum pink. I went with purple glitter. Because, well, glitter.

That evening, the hotel had a wine tasting event. A white and two reds from a local winemaker. He was a short man with an egg shaped head who droned on and on about grape varieties.

Miriam was ensconced in a chair next to the fireplace. She'd added lip liner about three shades darker than her magenta lipstick and powder, which had settled into the heavy lines of her face. Her hair was scooped into a severe bun and she watched everyone through hooded eyes. I could easily imagine her the matriarch of a mob family. Something told me that for all her bonhomie, she was not a woman to be trifled with.

I wandered over, a glass of chardonnay in one hand. It was too oaky for my taste, but it was free. "Any more letters?" I asked Miriam.

"Unfortunately, no."

I lifted a brow. "Unfortunately?"

She grinned impishly, that wide, magenta mouth curling like a joker's. "They do liven things up, do they not?"

I thought of the death threat Angie Tupper got. "I wouldn't put it that way, exactly."

"I'm an old woman. I get my enjoyment where I can." She cackled wildly.

I gave her a forced smile. The woman was odd. "Great. Well, I need to say hello to some friends. Nice seeing you again." I drifted over to Larry Tupper who stood alone, staring out the window to the rapidly darkening sea. His half-full glass dangled, forgotten, from one hand.

"How's Angie doing?" I asked.

He started. "Oh. She's fine. Resting." A muscle worked in his jaw. "We should have never come here."

"Why did you? There must be plenty of other romantic places to choose from."

"We got a deal online. Never could resist a deal. I think we're going to leave tomorrow." He leaned closer, lowering his voice. "I heard someone else got a letter."

I wondered if he'd heard about mine. "Really? Who?"

He nodded toward the other side of the room where a young couple sat on a leather loveseat, heads close together. She had chestnut colored hair piled in a wild up do and almond shaped eyes. She was pretty in a girl-next-door kind of way. The young man had ice blond hair and a tattoo up one side of his neck. He looked like he belonged in a 90s rap video.

"Newlyweds. They're on their honeymoon."

"What an odd couple," I mused. "Do you know what their letter said?"

"No. I just overheard him yelling at the manager about it. Thought you might want to know."

"Oh, I do. Thanks, Larry."

He nodded and went back to staring out the window. Something felt off about him, but I didn't have any idea what to say. Instead, I wandered to another window and did some staring of my own.

Cheryl brought over new glasses filled with ruby red liquid. "Pinot," she said. "It's tolerable."

I drained my glass of chardonnay and exchanged it for the pinot. She was right. Tolerable was the word. Barely.

"I was just talking to Larry." I explained what he'd told me about the young couple and their letter. "I want to talk to them."

"Are you sure that's a good idea? They don't look very friendly."

"This is important. We need to know what that note said."

She groaned. "Why? Why must you always get involved in these things?"

"I'm not getting involved."

She gave me a look. "Please."

"Fine. Whatever. The manager doesn't want to involve the police, so I'm determined to find out who the letter writer is."

"And then what?" she asked, propping one hand on her hip.

"Well, I hadn't planned that far."

"Of course not," she muttered.

I gave her an irritated look. Sometimes she could be a stick-in-the-mud when it came to investigating. "Come on. Let's go talk to them."

She followed me over to where the young couple still huddled near the bar. I stuck out my hand. "Hi, I'm Viola. This is my best friend, Cheryl."

The young man glared at me, the scowl twisting his face from moderately handsome to downright unattractive. "Someone said you were lesbians."

I could almost hear Cheryl growling. "You got a problem with that?" she snapped.

He had the grace to look embarrassed. "Uh, no. Just wondered why you were pretending to be friends."

"We're not pretending anything, not that it's any of your business," I said tartly.

"Sorry about Kevin. He can be an ass sometimes." The girl gave me a wobbly smile. Up close her eyes were an amazing aquamarine. I wondered if the color was real, or aided by contacts. "I'm Belle."

"Listen," I said, perching on a chair across from them. "I don't mean to be nosey, but I heard you got a poison pen letter, too."

"Too?" Belle asked, eyes wide.

Cheryl sat down next to me. "Viola and I got a letter the day we arrived. Accused us of being lesbians." She gave Kevin a pointed look. He glanced away.

"Then we got a second one today," I said. "It was a nasty threat."

Belle sagged in her seat, seeming almost relieved. "This morning the manager asked us if we'd gotten a letter. We said no, because we hadn't. But after lunch, there *was* a letter."

"What did it say?" I asked.

"What does it matter?" Kevin snarled.

"It might matter a lot," I said. "It could speak to who the letter writer is."

Belle reached over and gripped Kevin's hand. "It accused Kevin of being a drug dealer. Which is ridiculous."

He certainly looked like someone who might be familiar with breaking the law. "Have you ever been involved in drugs?" I asked.

"I grow pot totally legally," he said. "Got a license and everything. Never been involved in hard drugs."

"I don't understand why someone would write something so mean," Belle said, tearing up.

Although technically the letter had been spot on, there was nothing illegal in what Kevin did for a living. Not in Oregon. "Probably just a stab in the dark. That's usually what these things are about. Some jerk just wanting to upset people." I reached over and patted her hand. "I think it's time I had a talk with the manager."

"Already did that," Kevin said. "She won't do anything. Just makes excuses and offers to comp stupid stuff. As if I need a free mini bottle of rum. Give me a free fifth of the good stuff, then we'll talk."

"Is that so?" She hadn't offered to comp Cheryl and me anything. "Well, I'll have a word with her anyway. It might be time to bring the police in."

Belle paled. "Do you really think that's necessary? If this is a prank, surely whoever it is will give up and go away."

"Maybe. Maybe not. But if we don't go to the police and something happens..." I trailed off. Poor Belle looked likely to keel over in a dead faint. Why was she also against getting the police involved?

Chapter 5

"Maybe Belle's got a secret past as a double agent for the Kremlin and that's why she doesn't want the police involved," I said as I swiped my key card in the lock. "Or maybe she's in Witness Protection."

Cheryl rolled her eyes. "Your imagination is running away again."

I turned and shot her a dirty look. "You'd think, as a writer, *your* imagination would be a little more active."

She snorted and I turned my attention back to the door. As I stepped across the threshold, I noticed another red envelope lying on the floor. I leaned over to pick it up. "Oh, yay. The Poison Pen has struck again."

Cheryl peered over my shoulder. "We sure are popular."

"No kidding." I moved further into the room so she could get past me and pried open the flap. The pink heart inside was pretty. The words were not. "Get a load of this: That boyfriend of yours is cheating on you. He's not where he says he is."

"Well, it's not for me. I don't have a boyfriend." Cheryl frowned. "And I can't imagine Lucas cheating on you. He's not that smarmy."

"You could have a boyfriend if you wanted one," I hinted.

Cheryl ignored me. Apparently we were still pretending that she wasn't half in love with Astoria's hottest homicide detective. "What do you suppose the writer means by Lucas not being where he says he is?"

"I'm guessing whoever it is wants me to think Lucas is in a hotel room getting it on with some floozy or something."

"Floozy?" Cheryl giggled. "You've been writing Westerns for too long."

"Yeah, well, there's an easy way to prove the letter writer wrong." I hit Facetime on my phone. Within seconds Lucas's face came into view. His dark hair, peppered with gray, was damp and a little rivulet of water ran down his high cheekbone. Steam billowed from an open door behind him. The minute he saw my face, his gray eyes lit up.

"Hey, gorgeous," his gravelly, slightly accented voice gave me the shivers. "How's the hotel? Are you enjoying yourself?"

"Had an amazing massage today. And just came back from a wine tasting. We're going out for dinner pretty soon, but I wanted to say hi. Guess you got out of the airport." The letter writer had been right about a hotel, but it didn't mean anything.

"I told them they could call me when a flight was ready. I was going to stay at a hotel until they got their act together. One of the perks of being semi-famous, I guess."

"Which hotel?" Was I being too obvious?

"The Royale in New York. It's not bad. Let me give you a tour." He walked me through the bedroom and bathroom. He even pulled open the mini bar. "See. Already decimated." He chuckled. "You should see the view." His eyes lit up like a kid at Christmas. "Let me show you." He strode over to the window and yanked back a pair of beige curtains. Then he held up his phone so I could get a good look at the lights twinkling across the city. Even with the snow fall, no one could mistake that skyline for anything but New York.

The rush of relief was almost palpable. I felt silly for doubting him. "That's amazing."

"Isn't it? I guess if you've gotta be snowed in somewhere, New York's the place to do it."

"How's it looking for V-Day?" I asked, unable to keep the hope out of my voice.

"There's still a couple days, so fingers crossed. The storm should pass over tonight and hopefully I can get out tomorrow."

"I'll keep my fingers crossed. Love you." Those words were still a new thing for us and I felt a little giddy saying them.

"Love you more."

"I notice you didn't tell him about the note," Cheryl said as I hung up.

"No sense getting him worried. Clearly someone is just trying to cause trouble. I mean, that's what poison pen nonsense is about right? It's not about truth."

"Sure, okay. But what is this person trying to achieve? I mean, so far it's just been a lot of nonsense and a couple veiled threats. You've gotten the most letters. Are they after you?" She looked a little freaked out by the thought.

"I doubt it. I mean, how do we know some of the others haven't gotten more than one letter? Maybe we've been out of our room more, so more opportunity? Who knows! What I do know is that I'm starving. Let's go eat."

"Dining room downstairs?" Cheryl asked.

"Naw. Let's hit Newport. There's a restaurant there that I'm dying to try."

# # #

Café Miranda was a quaint little place with a view of Newport Bay. The shingles on the upper half of the building were weather beaten to a muted gray. The lower half was concrete and painted in a yellow so bright it outshone the sun.

Inside, the décor was 1950s diner, complete with vinyl covered booths and a jukebox in the corner. License plates from every state in the union were tacked onto the walls. It was one of those breakfast all day sorts of places. So I ordered blueberry pancakes with a side of bacon. Cheryl went with a boring Cobb salad made with fresh, Pacific Northwest salmon.

"Look," Cheryl hissed after the waitress—a woman in her fifties with bouffant hair and a pink uniform—brought us our food. "It's the Tuppers."

Sure enough, Angie and Larry sat a few booths over from us, eating silently. Larry had the hang-dog expression of someone who'd recently been chastised. Angie ignored him and focused completely on her food.

"Not exactly the sort of place I expect to see *her*," Cheryl whispered.

"No kidding," I whispered back. "Definitely expected her to prefer a posh place like Poisson." Poisson was a French style seafood place just a few doors down. One of those places with four dollar signs on the review sites and sauces with unpronounceable names. Since I couldn't eat seafood, I'd no interest in trying it.

"Did you tell them about this place?"

I shook my head. "Maybe Jeremiah told them. That's his job, right? To recommend places."

"I guess. It's just…weird."

"People have a way of surprising you." But Angie didn't seem to be enjoying either the ambiance or her food. And Larry looked plain miserable. Weird, indeed.

Shéa MacLeod

Chapter 6

It was still dark out when I woke to loud talking and thuds along the hall. A bleary squint at the clock revealed it was nearly five in the morning. Unacceptable.

On the other side of the room, Cheryl curled blissfully on her side, snoring lightly. I shot her a scowl and staggered from bed, my brain still muzzy as I shrugged on the hotel-supplied robe and slippers. Cracking open the door, I popped my head out.

Two uniformed cops stood guard at a room near the end of the hall. The manager—Anna Kettrick—dressed in jeans and a fleece pull-over, wrung her hands as she peered into the room. A man and a woman in blue windbreakers strode down the hall, chatting in low voices. As they approached the room, two men in rumpled suits stepped out and let them in. The back of the blazers read "OSP CID." I was guessing they were from the Oregon State Police's Criminal Investigation Division. How'd they get here so fast? And who was dead?

The men in suits said something to Anna. She nodded and tromped down the hall toward me, head down, chewing her lower lip.

As she passed, I called out, "Anna, what's going on?"

She glanced up, startled. "Oh, Ms. Roberts. Did we wake you? I'm so sorry. Please, go back to sleep."

"Don't give me that nonsense. Someone's dead."

She paled and glanced back down the hall to the men in suits who were now eyeing us intently. "How do you know?"

"Why else would the police be here? And the crime scene investigators?" Actually, if I thought about it, there were a lot of reasons: burglary, bomb threats, missing person. But this just *smelled* of murder. I could feel it in my gut.

"It's Belle Holland."

For a minute, I couldn't place the name. Then I remembered the girl with the amazing aquamarine eyes. "That sweet young newlywed?"

Anna nodded. "Her husband, Kevin, went out to get ice. And when he came back, she was dead." A tear slid down her pale cheek. "Poor kid."

"He went out for ice in the middle of the night?" And how long had he been gone? Must have been quite a trip.

"Well, they *are* newlyweds. I mean were." She choked back a sob.

"How did she die?"

"I'm not sure. I couldn't see anything. The police wouldn't let me in the room." She shuddered. "Not that I want to know."

"Was it murder?"

"Interesting that you should ask, Miss..." The voice that interrupted was masculine and deep with a smoker's rasp.

I turned to face the two rumpled looking men in suits. Detectives, obviously. I hadn't even seen them approach. The older of the two men—the one that had spoken—was tall and rangy with gray hair, a long, lugubrious face, and a small scar across the top of his nose. The younger man was six inches shorter, several pounds heavier, with thinning, medium brown hair and small, beady eyes. He remained silent but watched us closely.

"Ms. Roberts. Viola Roberts. And you are?"

"Detective Joe Meyers. This is my partner, Detective Fletcher." They both flashed their badges.

"What happened to Belle?" I asked.

"You knew the victim." Detective Meyers's face was blank, but his shrewd eyes gave him away. He was nobody's fool.

"I met her last night at the wine tasting," I said. "She was upset. She had just received one of the poison pen letters."

Fletcher's brow went up. "Poison pen letters?"

I whirled on Anna. "You didn't tell them?"

"It can't have anything to do with this." Anna clutched her hands together so hard, her knuckles turned white and I was half afraid she'd snap her fingers in half.

"Let us be the judge of that, ma'am." Detective Meyers gave her a stern look. "Now, about those letters?"

I told him about the three letters I'd gotten and about how inaccurate they were. I also told her about my conversations with Miriam, the Tuppers, and Belle. "The author seems to be targeting women."

"Oh, really?" Detective Meyers didn't say anything else. I was betting he'd already put two and two together, but he clearly wanted to see if I'd done it, too.

"So far, only women have received letters. Even though Belle and Angela are both with their husbands, the letters I saw were aimed at the women specifically. Not the men. I don't know why, but whoever is writing these letters, I think he, or she, hates women. Wants to torture them. Destroy their happiness."

"Well, isn't that interesting. Don't you think that's interesting, Fletcher?" Meyers didn't even look at his partner, but kept his focus on me.

"What happened to Belle?" I demanded. "Was she murdered?"

"Why would you say that?" Meyers asked.

"Because, like I told you, the letter Belle got was a threat. Maybe the letter writer decided to carry it out." Though from what I knew of poison pen writers, they didn't usually carry things out. They just liked to stir the pot, so to speak.

"We don't believe it was murder," Fletcher said.

"You think she killed herself over that stupid letter?" I could hardly believe it, but I remembered how scared Belle had been. How emotional. Maybe she suffered from depression and the letter had pushed her over the edge? What did I know about her, after all?

"It looks that way, I'm afraid," Detective Meyers admitted. He still eyeballed me with suspicion, but it seemed more like regular cop suspicion than anything personal.

"That poor woman," I muttered. "And a newlywed, too. Her husband must be devastated."

"Seems that way," Fletcher said. Meyers shot him a glare.

It seemed that way, huh? But what did we really know about Kevin? Could he have used the letter to cover up the murder of his wife? Or had Belle really been that fragile? I needed to talk to the man. The sooner the better.

# # #

"That's terrible." A scowl line crossed Lucas's forehead. The image was a little glitchy this morning, but not terrible. "They really think she killed herself?"

"That's what the detective's said at stupid o'clock this morning." I stirred sugar into my coffee. Outside the rain had started again. "Not sure I believe it."

"Let me guess. You think the husband was involved."

41

"It's possible," I admitted.

"You're not going to leave this to the police, are you?"

"There's someone sending nasty letters to people and one of those letters got someone killed. It's not right. And I'm not sure the police are taking the poison pen thing seriously." I wasn't sure they weren't taking it seriously, either, but I didn't like to leave things up to chance.

"At least be careful."

"I'll do my best."

"Viola..."

"Have you got a flight out yet?" I asked, changing the subject.

He rubbed his forehead as if he had a headache. "Yes. I should be back in Portland by eight tonight. I'll drive over in the morning. I hope Cheryl won't be too upset."

I repressed a little squeal of excitement that we'd be able to spend Valentine's Day together. "Oh, Cheryl can handle it."

"Cheryl can handle what?" Cheryl asked, dropping into the empty seat across the table from me. She looked half asleep.

"Lucas is driving down tomorrow. Your job as babysitter will be done."

"Thank goodness," she said as the waitress hurried over to pour her coffee. "Eggs over easy, please. Wheat toast and extra bacon on the side." The waitress left with the order and Cheryl eyed me over the rim of her cup. "I just heard about Belle. I do not want to spend the next few days tormenting the other guests."

I ignored her and focused on Lucas. "So, I'll see you tomorrow then."

He grinned. "It's a date." We bid each other goodbye and I hung up. "You're really okay with getting kicked out just before V-Day?"

"That was the point, right? I was just keeping you company until he could get here. Besides..." Her gaze slid away from mine. "I sort of have a date."

"What? Did Bat finally ask you out?" James "Bat" Battersea was the hottest detective on the Astoria police force. He'd been crushing on Cheryl for ages, but so far she'd rebuffed his advances.

Her cheeks pinkened. "It's not a big deal. Just a casual thing. We agreed if we were both free, we'd meet up for wine at Nina's."

Our friend, Nina, owned Astoria's only wine bar, Sip. It was our go to hang out, though I'd never seen Bat there. He seemed more of a beer guy.

"Excellent. You'll have to tell me everything."

Cheryl rolled her eyes. "There's not going to be anything to tell. It's just casual. Friends."

"My ass."

Her eyes narrowed. "Excuse me?"

"Did I say that out loud?"

She snorted. "Let me guess, you've got a list of suspects you want to interrogate this morning."

"Interview," I corrected. "What I really want to know is, did Belle truly commit suicide? And if so, was it really the letter that drove her to it?"

"And if that's the case?"

"Then the letter writer is essentially guilty of murder," I said grimly. "And I'm going to find out who did it."

Chapter 7

I found Kevin sitting on the same couch where I'd met him and his wife the day before. He wore the same clothes and sat hunched over, hands clasped between his knees. There was a blank expression on his face. Either he was in shock or he was a sociopath. It could go either way.

"I'm so sorry about Belle," I said, pulling up a chair. I wanted to sit where I could get a good look at his face.

He swallowed, Adam's apple bobbing in his narrow throat. "Thanks."

"Here, drink this. It'll help with the shock." I handed him a mug of hot chocolate liberally spiked with whiskey from the mini bar. He hadn't struck me as the tea type of guy.

He stared into the mug for ages before taking a sip. The boozy hot cocoa put a little color in his cheeks.

"The police seem to think she was so upset over the poison pen letter than she, ah..."

"Killed herself? That's stupid. Belle would never do that. We were happy..." He slumped against the back of the couch looking miserable. "I thought we were happy."

I eyed him carefully. He didn't have the manner I'd associate with someone who'd bumped off his wife recently. In fact, he seemed genuinely upset. Or maybe he was just a really good actor.

"Do you have any family I could call for you? Friends?"

His eyes flicked toward me and back to the mug. "Nobody nearby."

That was evasive as all get-out. I kept my expression neutral. "I'm sure they'd want to know regardless."

"I'll tell them. When I'm ready." His hand tightened on the mug.

"Fair enough." I laced my fingers together in my lap. "Belle was really upset over the letter yesterday."

"Wouldn't you be?" He sounded a little testy.

"Maybe. Except that I know these things tend to be a bunch of nonsense."

"It's not non-sense, though, is it? Belle's dead. And I don't believe for a moment she killed herself."

I leaned forward. "I don't either."

That piqued his interest. He glanced up at me, eyes wide. "Really?"

"Truly. Did anything happen last night after the wine tasting?"

"Nothing unusual. We had dinner here at the hotel. In the dining room. We shared a bottle of wine. Belle really loved the pinot." He choked up a little at the memory, but managed to pull himself together. "Miriam stopped by to congratulate us, which I thought was nice. She sat down and chatted with Belle for a bit. Belle is—was—really into everything Los Angeles."

"Did Belle have any enemies? Anyone who might want to hurt her?"

"People loved Belle. She was so sweet, you know." He scrunched up his face a bit. "There was this one girl, though. Katie. They used to be best friends and then Katie stabbed Belle in the back. Spread all these nasty lies about her. Belle was totally devastated."

"I can imagine," I said soothingly. "What sort of lies?"

"Just stuff like Belle stole from this charity she worked for. Or that she was a racist and homophobic. As if. Belle loved people. *All* people. And she was totally into equality and stuff. She even got arrested at a protest last year."

I nodded. "Do you know what started the argument between Belle and Katie?"

He shrugged. "No idea. One minute they were BFFs and then next..." he slid a finger across his throat.

Interesting. A bust up between two friends, one who liked to tell lies, if Kevin was to be believed. Sounded like the type of person to write a poison pen letter. Except for the fact that if Katie and Belle were the same age, that would make them millennials. Not exactly the age group one associated with handwritten letters. Wouldn't they be more likely to text? Or plaster nonsense all over social media? Still, it wouldn't hurt to have a chat with Katie.

"Do you have Katie's phone number?" I asked.

"It's probably in Belle's phone, but the police took it."

Darn. "What's Katie's last name?"

"Murkin. Katie Murkin."

It was unusual enough maybe I could find her online. I thanked him and hurried to my room. Cheryl was packing her bags.

"You're sure in a rush to get out of here," I said tartly.

She gave me a smug smile. "I talked to Bat. We're confirmed for Valentine's Day."

"Unless there's a murder and he has to work."

Her face fell.

"I'm sure there won't be." I tried to sound reassuring. "Listen, I may have a lead on the poison pen writer." I told her about Katie and her supposed lies about Belle. "Sounds like a prime suspect for the writer, don't you think?"

"Sure. Except she's not here, is she? At least not at the hotel. Belle surely would have noticed her nemesis."

"No," I admitted. "Not as far as I know. Though she could be staying somewhere nearby. That's why I'm here. I'm going to Google her." I sat down at the desk and opened my laptop. I typed Katie's name into the search bar. The results were all over the place, so I pulled up the most popular social media site and searched there. There were four results. One lived in

Britain. One was clearly too old. That left two. And I was loathe to send a message that might get lost in some spam folder.

Another thought struck me and I pulled up Belle's profile. A search of her friends revealed no one named Katie Murkin. Of course, she'd probably blocked Katie after what went down. But it did reveal that Belle was from Arizona. Which meant Katie was probably from Arizona, too. Sure enough, one of the two Katie's was living in Phoenix. I sent her a friend request and a message explaining I was friends with Belle's husband (a slight exaggeration but necessary) and had she heard that Belle was dead? Katie accepted my request within seconds and then sent me a video chat request. I held back a smile and accepted.

Katie wasn't what I expected. Actually, I'm not sure what I expected, but she was a cute little thing with a pixie cut and more makeup than she actually needed. She wore a black top with sparkly letters half hidden beneath the edge of the screen.

The first thing out of her mouth was a string of cuss words followed by, "Are you sure she's dead?"

"Very sure."

"What happened?"

I explained briefly. I didn't tell her about the poison pen letters or anything like that. Just that she'd been found dead, possibly a suicide. "Kevin said you used to be friends. I thought you might want to know."

"Well, serves her right."

I blinked. "Excuse me?"

Her expression hardened, leeching away much of the prettiness. "She stole my boyfriend."

"But she's married. I mean was."

"Yeah. To my boyfriend."

That was a surprise. "You dated Kevin?"

"Yep." She leaned back, her chair creaking heavily. "For two months. Then I introduced him to my best friend and he dumped me so fast it's a wonder I didn't get whiplash."

"So, he dumped you? I thought Belle stole him."

"Well yeah. I mean, he wouldn't have dumped me if that witch hadn't have put it out there, ya know?"

I wasn't sure I did, but I didn't want to antagonize her. She was my best bet for poison pen writer. "Is that why you told people she stole and stuff?"

She leaned forward, the chair creaking again. "You bet. She deserved it after what she did."

"But did she really do those things? Steal from the charity? Say racist stuff?"

"Naw." Katie waved her hand. "Unfortunately, she was as goody goody as they come. Not a racist or homophobic bone in her body and she'd rather cut off her own hand than steal anything."

"So you just made it all up to what? Hurt her?"

"Yeah. Of course. Like I said, she deserved it." She crossed her arms and glared at me stubbornly. Even with her former friend dead, she still held on to the anger. Maybe it was easier than grief.

"Did you ever send her a letter or anything?"

"What, like write on paper?" She snickered. "That's old people stuff. It was all online. Social media. That's where you can really crucify a person. Destroy 'em, ya know?"

Wow. She was quite a piece of work. But unfortunately I was beginning to suspect she wasn't the culprit. "So, it was public? Like anyone could see what you said and how she responded?"

"Sure. Why?"

"Well," I decided to tell her and see how she reacted. "Somebody sent her a pretty nasty letter."

"That's awesome! More power to 'em. What'd they say?"

"Not sure," I lied. "I just know it wasn't very nice."

Katie lifted one eyebrow. A silver ring glinted in the light. "Did she off herself over it?"

"The police aren't saying."

"Pity. Still, bitch deserved it."

What a nasty piece of work. No sympathy whatsoever. And all over a guy she dated a whopping two months. "It's sunny here," I lied. "Should be a nice day. How's the weather where you are?"

"Insanely hot. Eighty already and it's only ten."

We said our goodbyes and logged off.

"What was that about the weather?" Cheryl asked. "It's raining."

"Yeah, but she wouldn't know that unless she was here. If she was lying and she was here, she might let something slip. But I don't think she's lying. I think she really is in Phoenix." I pulled up a weather site. "Yep. It's eighty. Just like she said."

"She could have pulled up a site like you did," Cheryl pointed out.

"Sure. But she didn't have time."

"She could have guessed. I mean, it's Phoenix. Isn't it always hot there?"

I closed the laptop. "True. But I don't think she's the letter writer. She's into social media. She knows that's how you destroy a person's reputation. I mean, that's where bullies go now to hurt their victims. Online. This letter writer...that's old school stuff. This is someone who loves the written word. And also loves to hurt people in a very personal way."

"Okay, so now what?" She wrapped her flip flops in a plastic bag and tucked them neatly in her suitcase.

"Now I need to figure out if Belle's death really was suicide. Or if it was murder. Until that happens, there's not much I can do about solving it." I ignored Cheryl's eye roll. "What I can do is focus on the letter writer. I need to talk to the manager. I think she might have what I need."

Chapter 8

"I'm not sure I can give you those." Anna Kendrick wrapped a strand of blond hair around her finger. There were dark circles under her eyes and her face had a pinched look that came of too much stress and lack of sleep. A half empty coffee cup with a smudge of coral lip gloss sat next to her elbow. "I've got to think of the privacy of my guests."

"Listen," I said, propping my fists on my hips. "One of your guests is dead. Another one of them is sending nasty letters. I think privacy might be overrated here."

"You're not the police," she said stiffly.

"No, I'm not. But the police don't care, do they? They think Belle was just an unhinged lunatic who offed herself and that the letters are a joke. They're not taking this seriously, but you and I? We know better, don't we?"

She glanced down, picking at her cuticle. "Maybe..."

"Come on."

She sighed and her shoulders fell. "Okay. I mean, yeah, something bad is going on. But shouldn't we leave it to the police?"

"Until when? Another one of your guests dies? Do you know what will happen to your occupancy then?"

She blanched. "Oh, no."

I managed to repress a gloat. "See, guests will stop coming. Occupancy will drop. Then where will you be?"

She buried her face in her hands. "Unemployed."

"Exactly." I hoped she was finally getting it.

She let out a shaky breath. "Okay. Give me a minute." She disappeared into the office behind the desk. I could hear the rustle of papers and file folders. Then she reappeared with several papers in her hands. "These are all the registration forms for the guests. Nobody's checked out since the letters started."

Which meant whoever was sending them had to be staying at the hotel. Or near enough they could get to the hotel easily without anyone noticing. "Are there any other hotels nearby?"

She shook her head. "Nearest one's in Newport."

It was possible, but unlikely. That was quite a trip for someone to make. Plus, the first letter had been on hotel stationary. "What about houses?" With those websites these days, anyone could rent out a house or a room to complete strangers.

"There's a condo, but it's almost five miles away. I know there are a couple houses back up in the hills, but I wouldn't think anyone there could be involved. We're very remote. My staff would have noticed anyone who didn't belong."

"What about staff? Do you have samples of their handwriting?"

"I looked at the nasty letters and the handwriting isn't familiar, but I do have notes and whatnot from staff. You can look at them." She handed me a small stack of post its and notebook paper. Casual scribblings from the employees of the hotel.

I nodded and began shuffling through the papers. I'd brought my own letters for comparison. All three had clearly been written by the same person. I had no idea if the spidery handwriting was the person's regular handwriting, or if it was some attempt at disguise. But there were still things people couldn't hide. I was no expert, but I was hoping something would jump out at me.

I laid out the poison pen letters and then carefully compared them to the employee notes. No matches. Next I moved to the registrations. It was difficult to tell as there wasn't much handwriting. Make, model, and license plate of the car. Name, address, and signature. That was it.

The first registration sheet was made out in heavy block letters. Absolutely impossible to compare. The signature, however, was definitely more of a scrawl. Although I doubted it was the letter writer, I set the sheet aside. It could be an attempt to disguise the person's handwriting. The next one was all round letters and extra swirls. Very feminine. And very unlike the poison pen letters. I put it on the reject pile.

And so it went until I had a stack of rejects and just two registrations on the "possible" pile. I handed Anna the rejects.

"You think it's one of them?" she asked, nodding to the two possibles.

"Maybe. Could you make copies of these two for me?"

She winced, but did as I asked. With the still warm photocopies tucked in my pocket, I headed back upstairs to my room. Cheryl was done packing.

"You leaving now?" I asked.

"Naw. I'll wait until Lucas gets here tomorrow. I'm not about to leave you alone. Not with a crazy person on the loose."

"Much appreciated," I said dryly.

She ignored my snark. "Any luck?"

I handed her the two registrations. "I can't be sure, but it could be one of these."

She carefully perused the first one. "This is Larry."

"I know."

She frowned. "Could be his regular handwriting, or an attempt at disguise."

"My thought exactly."

"And this one..." she squinted. "This one is Miriam? The old lady? Are you serious?"

"Look how similar the writing is. She's old, not senile. She could easily have written those letters."

Cheryl sank into a chair next to the window. "There is something else you may not have considered." Outside, rain peppered the window panes. The dark skies turned the sea into molten lead.

"That the letter writer never filled out a registration form? Yeah. That's a possibility." After all, only one guest signed the form. In a couple situation, that meant the second person didn't sign anything. I had Larry's form, but Angie hadn't filled anything out. "There's also the possibility that the writer is someone who works here."

I mulled that over. "No, I don't think so. The letters didn't start until after you and I arrived. There was never been a problem before, and Anna says they haven't hired anyone new in over a year." I paused, realizing what I'd said.

"You think our arrival triggered something?"

"That's what I'm wondering. If that's true, then it *could* be someone who works here. But why? Why you and me."

"You mean, why you?" she said.

"What do you mean?"

She rolled her eyes. "Viola, you're being dense. Those letters weren't for me. They were for you. Accusing Lucas of cheating. Why would I care about that other than to be outraged for your sake? Accusing us of being lesbians. Again, why would I care? I haven't got a boyfriend. No one would care if I was a lesbian. But it might cause problems for you."

"The death threat wasn't specific." I was grasping at straws.

"No, but based on the other two letters, I'm guessing that one was for you, too."

Well that put things in a new perspective. "How am I going to get writing samples from everyone?"

"I don't know. Get creative."

I groaned. This was getting to be too much. Still, I couldn't give up. Poor Belle deserved more.

"I still need to find out if Belle's death was a murder or a suicide. I'm going to call that Detective."

Chapter 9

Detective Meyers was decidedly unhelpful. In fact, he hung up on me. Fletcher was no better. He refused to take my call. So, I did the only other thing I could think of. I called Bat.

"Detective Battersea."

"Hey Bat."

He let out a growling sound. "What do you want, Viola?"

I told him about Belle's death. "All I want to know is, did she kill herself? Or did someone else do it?"

"And why do you want this information?"

"Just to settle my mind," I said innocently.

He snorted. "You're investigating again, aren't you?"

"I don't know what you mean."

"At least you're Meyers's problem. Give me a few. I'll get back to you." He hung up without saying goodbye.

A few minutes later the phone rang. "Hello, Bat."

"Viola. I talked to Meyers. She was smothered, but there was no struggle."

"What?" My mind whirled. "That can't be suicide. Struggle or no struggle."

"No it can't. Meyers thinks she was drugged and then probably a pillow put over her face. He's waiting on the results of the blood test."

"Are they going to arrest Kevin?"

"Who?"

"Her husband," I said.

"What makes you think her husband did it?"

"Isn't it always the husband?" I asked.

"Often, but not always."

"Well, I'm thinking it definitely was this time."

"Why?" he asked. "Why not the letter writer?"

"Because. The letter writer has handed out a lot of nasty notes, but not done anything actually violent. Plus, there was just something about the way Kevin looked at Belle that first night..."

"They're newlyweds, Viola. Why would he kill her?"

"I don't know, maybe he wanted her money?"

"She didn't have any."

"Well, there has to be a motive somewhere and I'm going to find out. Thanks, Bat."

He grunted and hung up. Again without a goodbye.

Me, I had other things to think about. Now I had two criminals to unmask. The letter writer and the killer. But I was sure Kevin killed Belle. I paused. Could he be the letter writer, too? His handwriting hadn't matched, but he could have disguised it. Used the letters to make everyone think Belle had killed herself. That had to be it. But first, I needed to know why.

# # #

I spent half the night hunched over my laptop mining every bit of Belle's information I could get my hands on. From social media, to random comments on cooking sites, I looked at absolutely everything with her name on it. Fortunately Belle Holland was an unusual enough name that it was fairly easy to determine if the Belle active on various sites was the Belle I was looking for.

Cheryl curled beneath the covers with one of those airline eye masks over her face, snoring gently. It was a delicate, feminine kind of snore that I found oddly soothing. It made the witching hour less lonely.

As the sun peered over the horizon, my eyes burned with fatigue. The screen in front of me blurred. Maybe it was time to go to bed. Lucas would be here soon.

And then I found it.

I nibbled on the edge of my thumb. What did this mean? It had to be important. Had to be.

I quickly made screen prints and saved them to my desktop. I didn't want to wake Cheryl. Not yet. It was just past seven in the morning. People would be getting up soon. And I was in desperate need of sleep. I could continue my investigations shortly. Just a quick catnap.

Shéa MacLeod

Chapter 10

I woke to the smell of coffee and bacon. I sat up, rubbing sleep from my eyes. "Have I died and gone to heaven?"

"Not dead. But definitely heaven." The mattress dipped as Lucas sat down next to me.

He was warm and solid and I wrapped myself around him, tucking my head against his shoulder. "You're here."

He kissed the top of my head. "You bet. Where else would I be? Tomorrow is Valentine's Day, and you are my Valentine."

I knew Lucas wasn't that into V-Day, but he knew I was. He got so many brownie points for wanting to make it special for me.

He picked up a piece of bacon and held it for me to nibble. "I figured room service was the way to go."

"You figured right." I frowned and glanced around the room. "Where's Cheryl?" Her suitcase was gone.

"She left about an hour ago. Right after I got here. Seems she has big plans tomorrow and wants to visit the salon today."

Of course she did. I settled back against him. Then sat bolt upright, nearly whacking him in the chin with my head. "What time is it?"

"A little after nine. Why?"

"Fiddlesticks!"

He looked at me askance. "Fiddlesticks? Seriously?"

"What? My mother says it. It sort of stuck." I rummaged through drawers, grabbing clothes willy nilly. "I hope it's not too late."

"Too late for what?"

I stopped, clutching a pair of jeans to my chest. "I'm not sure, to be honest. But I need to talk to one of the other guests. About the murder."

"Whoa. Slow down. Check out isn't until eleven."

"But she could leave at any moment." I dashed into the bathroom and ripped off my pajamas then yanked on clothes. Coffee. I needed coffee. My eyes ached and my brain hurt.

I exited the bathroom to find Lucas holding out a mug of fragrant, dark brew. With a cry of joy I took it from him and took a long, blissful sip. "You rock. Now, where was I?"

"You need to talk to someone. About the murder," he prompted.

"Right." I charged toward the door, only half noticing I was still barefoot.

Lucas grabbed the back of my sweater and yanked me to a stop. "Slow down. Show me what you've got."

I blinked. "What?"

"You obviously found something, but aren't quite sure what it means. Before you run off half-cocked, slow down and show me."

He knew me so well. With a nod, I sank down in the desk chair and opened my laptop. I clicked on the image I'd saved. "I was researching Belle last night. Trying to figure out why someone would kill her."

"Any conclusions? Could the letter writer have killed her?"

Had I remembered to brush my hair? I shook my head. Nope. Definitely not. "I don't think it's related at all. I think the killer took advantage of the poison pen situation to hide the murder. In fact, Belle's letter may not have even been from the poison pen writer. I never saw it. Belle only told me about it."

"Okay, so what does this article," he pointed at the image on the screen, "have to do with it?"

I drew a deep breath. "While searching through social media, I found that Belle has a maternal uncle, Patrick Wallace. Belle is…was…as far as I can tell, his only living relative."

"Okay." He pulled up an armchair and sat down. "Is this Patrick Wallace rich?"

"Very."

"So, Belle is his likely heir."

"I have no way of knowing for sure," I admitted. "But my guess is that she is."

"All right. So, I repeat, what's this article have to do with anything?"

"See this woman?" I tapped the screen.

Lucas nodded. "Interesting sense of style."

"Indeed. She's staying at this hotel. Her name is Miriam Bartolomey. She's from Paraguay."

"Again, interesting, but—."

"Patrick Wallace retired to Paraguay three years ago," I interrupted.

Lucas's eyes lit up. "Really? Still, Paraguay is a big country. Could be a coincidence."

"Sure," I agreed. "But that man standing next to Miriam in the photo? That's Patrick Wallace."

# # #

"Where's Miriam Bartolomey?"

Jeremiah's head jerked up. He gave me a puzzled look. "Why, she checked out early this morning. It was odd. She was supposed to stay through tomorrow, but..."

"Where'd she go?" I demanded.

"Um, she had one of those ride share cars pick her up. I heard her tell the driver to head for the Newport Municipal Airport."

Lucas frowned. "There's an airport in Newport?"

"Of course, sir," Jeremiah said. "It's very small. Charter services and private planes mostly."

"Fiddlesticks, she's getting out of Dodge. We've got to stop her." I charged for the front door of the hotel.

Lucas grabbed my arm. "Perhaps we should call the police?"

"Fine. We can do it on the way."

"And get shoes." He glanced down.

"I'm wearing—oh, slippers." I grimaced. "You warm up the car and I'll be out in a minute." I ran for the room where I swapped out slippers for shoes. I grabbed my purse and jacket, then ran to the parking lot where Lucas had pulled the car around to the entry. I hopped in and he took off in a squeal of tires.

"I've got Detective Meyers on the phone." He handed me his cell.

I quickly outlined what I'd found out and my suspicions about Miriam Bartolomey. "There's no doubt in my mind she killed Belle Holland."

"And what would be her motive?" he asked dryly. "She's an old woman. So what if she knows Mrs. Holland's estranged uncle?"

"From what I saw in that picture, Miriam knows Belle's uncle in the very biblical sense. Patrick Wallace is a rich man and, according to the article, has been quite ill. I'll bet you a hundred bucks, Patrick left everything to Belle."

"Again, how does that effect Miriam?"

"Because I'm betting there's something in that will that benefits her, but only if Belle is dead."

He let out a long suffering sigh. "It's a long shot."

"Miriam left the hotel a day early."

"Maybe she had a good reason. People cancel their vacations early all the time."

I wanted to scream in frustration, but Lucas held out his hand. I slapped the phone in it. "Detective. This is Lucas Salvatore. Would you please find out what was in Patrick Wallace's will? Thank you." He hung up.

"So, what, all you have to do is ask?"

Lucas gave me a sly smile. "I know people."

I rolled my eyes. "Fine. Is he going to do it?"

"Yes. And if he finds anything, he'll meet us at the airport."

"That's not a lot of time," I muttered. The airport was only about thirty minutes away. Another thought struck. "What if the plane took off already? Jeremiah said Miriam left the hotel early this morning. She could be long gone by now."

"While you were inside I called the airport. There's a charter flight to San Francisco scheduled to leave in an hour. We'll catch her."

I held on to the edge of my seat, fingers digging into the leather as I willed the car to go faster. Finally Lucas pulled into the airport and screeched to a halt in front of a building attached to a hanger. Through the tall windows I could see a small waiting area.

Because the airport was so small and strictly for private charter flights, there was no security check point. I tumbled out of the car and ran for the waiting room, Lucas hot on my heels. Inside about half a dozen people sat calmly reading magazines and e-readers.

"Ladies and gentlemen, your charter flight to San Francisco departs in twenty minutes. Please prepare for boarding."

Everyone began gathering bags. I peered around trying to spot Miriam.

"There." Lucas pointed.

Miriam was seated close to the door to the tarmac. Clearly she was hoping to make a quick escape. I knew the moment she saw us. She looked at first surprised, then resigned. Then a strange, smug expression overtook her. Yeah, she was going to play this to the last.

"Hello, Miriam," I said.

She gave me a slow smile. Her magenta lipstick was smeared up in the creases of her mouth. It matched the chiffon scarf around her neck. "Viola. Fancy meeting you here. And is this your beau?"

"This is my boyfriend, Lucas, yes."

"How lovely. And so handsome." Miriam's eyes sparkled maliciously.

"We know you did it," I blurted.

"Did what, dear?"

"You murdered Belle Holland." I crossed my arms. Oops. I forgot to put on a bra.

Miriam laughed. "That poor girl at the hotel. How ridiculous. I'm an old woman. How could I possible murder anyone?"

"Easy," I said, sitting down across from her. "You drugged her."

"How would I do that?" She sat back placidly.

"According to Detective Meyers, the drug was in her glass of wine at dinner," Lucas said.

"And I talked to Kevin. The night Belle died, you sat with them at dinner for a bit. You could have easily slipped something in her drink then. After Kevin left for ice, you slipped into her room and pressed the pillow over her face until she stopped breathing. With the drugs in her system, there would have been no way she could have fought back against you."

"Prove it."

Man, I wanted to wipe the smug smile off her face. "I can't," I admitted, "but I'm sure the police can."

She snorted. "They have no reason to. What could possibly my motive?"

"Money."

I jerked my head up at the gravelly voice. "Detective Meyers."

He didn't look at me, but kept his gimlet gaze on Miriam. I noticed Detective Fletcher was also there and had worked his way around behind Miriam. Probably to stop her from bolting. Which would be silly except I've seen what octogenarians can do when they put their minds to it.

"Detective. Have you come to send me off?" Miriam asked.

"I've come to send you to jail for murder," Detective Meyers said grimly.

"Ridiculous," she snorted. "How would Belle's death benefit me?"

This time Meyers did glance at me. "Thanks to Ms. Roberts, we did a little digging. Seems Belle Holland was the only heir to one multi-millionaire named Patrick Wallace. The same Patrick Wallace you've been seeing for the past year. The same Patrick Wallace who is currently on his deathbed."

"What of it?" Miriam snarled.

"It seems there's a caveat in the will. Should Belle predecease Patrick, you get everything."

It was my turn to smile smugly. "You murdered Belle for Patrick's millions. And you used the poison pen letters to cover it up."

Detective Meyers cleared his throat. "Miriam Bartolomey, you're under arrest for the murder of Belle Holland."

Never had the sound of handcuffs snapping around a pair of wrists been more satisfying.

Shéa MacLeod

Chapter 11

"She didn't do it." Lucas set his phone on the bedside table.

I had been happily making myself a cup of coffee. It was officially Valentine's Day morning. The killer had been caught. It was over. And then the phone had rung. "Excuse me?"

"That was Meyers. Miriam Bartolomey killed Belle Holland. There's no doubt. But she didn't write the poison pen letters. She simply took advantage of them."

I sat down on the edge of the bed, careful not to slosh my coffee. "Dagnabbit. I was sure she'd done it all."

"We're back to square one."

"Not quite. Once I discovered the truth about Miriam, I never did follow up on the registrations." I told him about my handwriting comparison. "The only two that were suspicious were Miriam's and Larry Tupper's. Obviously we can rule out Miriam."

"It's shaky, but it doesn't hurt to try. Let's talk to Larry."

We dressed quickly and hurried downstairs. Jeremiah was at his usual post.

"I need to speak to Larry Tupper. What room are they in?" I asked.

"Oh, I'm sorry. The Tuppers have checked out."

Lucas and I exchanged glances. The frustration in his expression matched my own.

"Did they say where they were heading?" Lucas asked.

"Home, I imagine." Jeremiah shuffled some papers around. "They were supposed to stay through tomorrow, but changed their minds. Seems to be going around."

"It has to be Larry," I said. "His handwriting was similar to the letters. And why else would they leave early?"

"You don't know that," Lucas said with irritating logic. "They could have been called away for any number of reasons. A family emergency, for instance."

"You might be able to catch them," Jeremiah said helpfully.

"What do you mean?" I demanded.

"They checked out only a few minutes ago," Jeremiah said. "They're probably still in the back parking lot loading their car. I haven't seen them drive around yet."

"Viola, I thought you said Larry was sort-of a nice-guy. Why would he write those letters?" Lucas asked.

It was true. I couldn't imagine chatty, kindly Larry writing poison pen letters. Then a thought struck me. "Jeremiah, did you check the Tuppers in?"

"Yeah, I did."

"Do you remember which of them filled out the registration?"

Jeremiah frowned, tapping his pen on the desk, closing his eyes slightly as if to re-live the moment. "Mr. Tupper put the room on his credit card, but Mrs. Tupper filled out and signed the form."

I whirled back to Lucas, excitement fizzing through my veins. "She did it, Lucas. Angie Tupper wrote those letters."

"Are you sure?"

"Of course I'm sure. The handwriting of her signature matches. I mean, there were small differences, but those could be accounted for by her trying to disguise her writing. I know she did it." It explained a lot about how strange she was whenever I was around. Her sour attitude about everything including her husband. The poor man had been nothing but loving. "We've got to stop them."

We charged out the door and around the side of the building just in time to see a red sports car pull out of one of the parking spaces. As it zipped by, the driver window rolled down and Angie Tupper stuck her head out. She gave me a smile that would have frozen a lesser woman. She knew I was on to her and she wasn't scared. Nope, if her smile was anything to go by, she was amused. "Oh, Viola, I left you a little something. Hope you enjoy it."

And then the car was gone, out of the parking lot. "They're getting away!"

Lucas was already on his cell. "Don't worry. I'm calling Meyers."

With Meyers's assurance that he was on the job, there was nothing left for us to do but wait. It was only when I pushed open the door to our room that I spotted it. "Was that there before?" I asked.

Lucas glanced at the red envelop laying on the floor just inside the door. It was slightly to the side, so it could have been there. In our hurry we might not have seen it. Could Angie, for have slid it under the door before she left? Was this the thing she left for me?

"I'm not sure."

I leaned over and picked it up. Lifting the flap, I pulled out the card inside and read it out loud. "Has Lucas told you about us? Enjoy your Valentine's Day. While you can. XOXO." I lifted my eyebrow. "Care to explain?"

He sighed heavily. "We need to talk."

My stomach turned sour. Those were four words that never, ever boded well. Twenty years ago I'd said them to my now ex-husband right before I asked for divorce. Was this karma coming back to bite me in the backside?

"Fine. Talk." I tried to pretend I wasn't in the least bit worried.

"I have a stalker."

I blinked. "What?" Of all the things I imagined would follow those four words, his having a stalker wasn't one of them.

He took my hand and guided me to the bed. "It started about six months ago. At first it was online comments and emails to my agent and publisher. Then I started getting emails sent to my personal email address. About three months ago, letters and little gifts began arriving at my post office box and then at my home. I had to get the police involved."

"Why didn't you tell me?"

"Because I didn't want you to worry."

"And what if this stalker person had come after me?" I glared at him. "Come to think of it, the stalker *did* come after me. That's what the whole poison pen thing was all about, isn't it? It was about me. And you. I was the only one who got three, now four, letters. Everyone else got one, maybe two."

He rubbed the bridge of his nose. "It was the wrong choice, obviously. Keeping the truth from you. And I'm sorry about that. And I'm sorry that whoever it is has you in her sights now."

"Her? You mean Angie Tupper."

"Yes. The police have already determined the stalker is a woman. That's about all they know. With these letters…I'm betting it was Angie and hopefully they'll be able to prove that. Put her away for a while."

I stared down at the valentine. "You never saw her before?"

"Maybe. It's hard to say. I meet a lot of people at signings. And the whole online thing. She could have seen me on social media. You never know. She's clearly unhinged."

"Clearly." My tone was dry.

"Listen, I'm sorry I didn't tell you. I was just…I wanted to keep you out of it. Keep you safe."

I rolled my eyes. It was sort of sweet of him. "Next time, try telling me the truth?"

"I will." He kissed my cheek and plucked the note from my hand. "I'll send this and the other letters to the police in Portland. They're handling the stalker case. As soon as Meyers catches Angie, he'll turn her over to them."

"You sound awfully sure Meyers can catch her."

"He's a good cop," Lucas assured me. "I'm certain he'll find her. But in the meantime, I think I need to start teaching you how to protect yourself. Just in case."

"I suppose if anyone's an expert, you are." Lucas had been in the Israeli army. He could probably kill a guy twenty-six different ways with a ballpoint pen.

The phone rang. Lucas held it up so I could see the screen. Meyers.

"Hello, detective. What's the news?" Lucas asked. "Uh, huh. Great. Thanks." He hung up. "They caught her. They'll hold her in the local jail until the PPD can arrange a transfer."

Relief coursed through me. "So this is over?"

He leaned over and planted a quick kiss. "You better believe it. Now, let's forget about everything and enjoy the day. Deal?"

"Deal." Though I wasn't sure forgetting would be so easy.

#

The rest of the day proved as romantic and uneventful as the morning had been exciting and decidedly unromantic. Lucas had taken me to the bookstore in Depot Bay. After a couple hours digging through stacks of dusty used books, I'd discovered a wonderful collection of poetry and a couple of vintage cookbooks that were too good to pass up. Who doesn't need a dozen recipes for Jell-O molds?

After a walk on the beach, we had a candlelit dinner at The Bay House in Lincoln City. As the sun slipped beneath the horizon leaving a sky bathed in gold and salmon pink, we sipped our wine, enjoying the evening and each other's company.

"I have an idea," Lucas said, leaning closer. His eyes gleamed in the candlelight and I caught the faintest whiff of his aftershave. Something spicy and wild, a little like him.

"I'll bite."

"England."

My eyes widened. "What?"

"England. The London Book Fair is next month and I've been asked to speak. We should go. Put in an appearance. Then we can spend a week or two exploring the countryside. What do you say?" He grinned happily. "It'll be corpse free."

"No murders? Now that's an offer I find irresistibly romantic."

We both laughed. I just hoped it was one he could keep.

Read on for a sample of the next book in the Viola Roberts Cozy Mystery series,

The Remains in the Rectory

Chapter 1
Lost in Translation

Driving on the wrong side of the road is not something I'd recommend. Especially if you want to keep both your sanity and your relationship intact.

"Watch the hedgerow, Viola!" Lucas braced himself against the dashboard of the ridiculously small Peugeot, knuckles turning white as I took the curve a little too fast. The hedgerow loomed ominously close.

"Shut up," I snapped. "I'm trying to drive, here." I'd been driving nearly thirty years, after all. I should be getting the hang of it by now.

Whose idea was this, anyway? Renting a car in England. Driving out to the picturesque Cotswolds. It had all sounded so great until the realities of driving on the left set in and I nearly sideswiped a lorry. (An American would have said truck, not lorry, but I was trying really hard to get into the spirit of the thing. It wasn't my fault, really. Left hand driving just doesn't come naturally to a person.

My boyfriend, Lucas Salvatore, sat hunched in the passenger's seat of the small rental car, alternately cussing and praying. Lucas was a few years older than me, making him closer to fifty than forty. He was ridiculously handsome with his bronzed skin and dark hair lightly peppered with gray. Usually he was a calm and supportive partner, but frankly, he was getting on my last nerve. I was perfectly capable of figuring this driving thing out without killing us. Probably.

We were somewhere out on what the English refer to as a "B road." In the States, it would be a country lane: narrow, harrowing. Filled with tractors and the distinct possibility of ending up with a deer in your windshield. Or rather, since this was England, a sheep.

Lucas and I were both writers. He wrote best-selling thrillers which Hollywood eagerly turned into blockbuster movies starring that actor with the big nose. I wrote western historical romances with cowboys and mail order brides. I made an excellent living, but Hollywood wasn't knocking.

When Lucas had suggested attending the London Book Fair, I'd jumped at the chance to leave my sodden little town of Astoria, Oregon for the wildly exotic (and equally sodden) streets of London. Our plan after the fair was to tour the English countryside by car. Lucas wanted to find some unexplored English village to include in his latest novel. So that's how we found ourselves on a B road, out in the Cotswolds, with Lucas snippy, me snappy, and lorries trying to murder us.

"How far have we got to go?" I said between gritted teeth. My smartphone wasn't working even though the carrier had promised it would, and the GPS system had crapped out thirty minutes ago.

Lucas battled with a paper map for a minute. "A couple more miles and we'll hit the turn off to the Roman Road. Then it's a straight shot to Moreton-in-Marsh. We can get the A44 to Oxford from there."

Oxford. And civilization! I could hardly wait. Just a little farther and we'd be back on "A roads" with properly definitely lanes. I breathed a sigh of relief.

And then the skies, which had been dark and ominous all day, suddenly opened up and dumped rain on us. It was like a freaking monsoon. I turned the wiper blades on high, and still I could barely make out the road ahead. My hands ached from gripping the steering wheel so tight.

"There's a branch in the road up here somewhere," Lucas said. "Keep right."

I nodded, but didn't take my eyes off the road, even though at this point I could barely see it. The only thing keeping me out of the ditch was the hedgerow looming to my left, so close the occasional branch scraped the side of the car. I sure hoped Lucas bought extra insurance to cover the scratches. If not, it would be a good reminder for him not to bother me while driving in a country influenced by Romans. It was thanks to them that the entire country insisted on driving on the wrong side of the road. I suppose one didn't want to block one's sword arm. Because I'd seen so many sword-carrying Audi drivers.

We drove three more miles before I said, "Where's that fork we were supposed to take?"

Lucas shrugged. "We should have found it by now, but maybe it's further up?"

I kept going, a sick feeling in my stomach. There were no signs indicating where we were or how close the next town was. I could only see a few inches in front of the windshield. I was starting to think we'd be lost out here forever, wandering in the English wilderness.

"Stop being dramatic."

I slid my gaze toward Lucas who was shaking his head. I frowned. "I didn't say anything."

"No. But you were thinking it." His voice was lightly accented with a rumbly sexiness to it.

I pointedly ignored him. "We're low on gas."

"Petrol," he corrected in an annoying fashion. "Once we get out on the Roman Road we should be okay."

"If we can find the cursed thing," I muttered.

The Roman Road was exactly what it sounded like: an ancient road built by the Romans which had been paved over a few decades back and turned into an A road. It was straight as an arrow—more or less—rising up hills and falling down dales. It marched its way across the landscape, much like its builders had, once upon a time. Unfortunately, it was nowhere in sight and I was stuck winding around the narrow backroad feeling lost and claustrophobic with the hedgerows pressing in on either side.

I knew it was dumb, but I was desperate to get off the B road as soon as possible. So, I said the Lord's Prayer that the tractors were all at home avoiding the rain, and pressed down on the gas pedal. The car lurched as it sped up.

"There!" Lucas shouted, jabbing a finger to the right. Sure enough, an even narrower road led off to the right. I jerked the steering wheel hard and hit the road at full tilt. It bounced and jarred something awful, until I was able to slow down enough to not kill us.

"That wasn't exactly a fork," I pointed out.

"True," he admitted, "but it was the first gap I saw in that abominable hedgerow. This has to be the road. There's been nothing else."

I wasn't so sure. The rain was pouring buckets. Every now and then the tires made a desperate attempt to hydroplane. Fortunately, I'm from a state where it rains more often than not. This was a piece of cake for me. If the cake was full of nuts and lumps of baking soda.

The narrow lane—it could hardly be described as a road—wound its way through a copse of trees, around thickets of brush, across a stone bridge, and past fields of some kind or other. Green shoots stood stubbornly beneath the onslaught of rain. Up ahead I saw a figure swathed in a yellow rain slicker slogging alongside the road. He, or she, wore rubber boots of ordinary green and had the slicker hood up. One hand gripped a gnarled walking stick, though it seemed to be more for effect than out of necessity.

"Pull up alongside," Lucas urged. "Surely this person can give us directions."

I did as instructed and Lucas rolled down the window. "Pardon me!" His usually faint accent grew suddenly thicker and sounded more British than it usually did. It didn't escape my notice that he also used British phrasing instead of American, as he did back home.

The figure in the slicker stopped and turned to face us. Although the face was rough, wrinkled, and devoid of makeup, it was still of the feminine variety.

"What are you two doing way out here?" The accent was thick with the slightly nasal intonations of the Midlands. The voice itself was strong and low, but definitely female. "You get yourselves lost?"

"Something like that," Lucas said. I couldn't see his face, but I knew he was giving the woman his most charming smile. "We're trying to find the Roman Road."

"Oh, that's way back there." She waved vaguely in the direction we'd come. So we *had* missed the fork. Darn it. "Some two, three miles."

"Well, that's no good. We're low on petrol, you see. Is there a village ahead?" he asked.

"Oh, ay. There is that." She gave him a warm smile, but no further information. I felt like smacking the wheel in frustration, but Lucas remained his calm, charming self. Naturally.

"How far is it? Do you think?"

She squinted off into the rain, the lines around her eyes feathering out. "'Bout a mile, I'd say. Give or take."

"Well, that's perfect." Lucas flashed his pearly whites. "Is there a turn off or anything?"

"Just keep on this road and you'll come to it. Can't miss it."

"Can we give you a ride?" he asked.

I scowled at him, though he couldn't see. I did not need her dripping water all over the rental car. I could just see trying to explain mildew stains on top of the paint scratches.

"Thank you, no. Got to get my walk in, you see."

"Of course. Thank you."

She nodded as Lucas rolled the window up and I put the car back in "drive." I frowned at the gas gauge. I sure hoped we had enough gas for a mile "or so." The gas light had been on for some time.

Just as the engine started sputtering, we rolled out of the woods and into a village. A small sign, impossible to read in the downpour, marked the outskirts. Such as they were. Stone buildings stood sentinel on either side of the narrow lane, blurred by rain, leaning against each other as if for support against the storm.

"We're not getting much further and I don't see a gas station," I said.

"Petrol station. It's fine. There's a pub. Pull in there."

Sure enough, there was one of those half-timbered old buildings with a sign swinging out front and lights burning brightly. A small parking lot to the side could hold about three cars. And lucky us, there was a spot empty. I pulled in just as the engine finally died.

Lucas grinned. "Perfect timing."

I glared at him. "If we hadn't gotten lost, it would have been fine."

"And whose fault is it we got lost?"

"Well," I said with a glare. "You were the navigator."

"Come on, Viola," he laughed. "This is an adventure. Let's see where it takes us." He climbed out of the car cutting off any reply I might have made.

With a sigh I climbed out, too, ducking my head against the onslaught of wind and rain. Lucas grabbed my hand and we ran to the pub side by side. Lucas stopped to jerk open the door and we hurried out of the cold and into the warm, steamy building.

To my left was an old, stone fireplace where flames danced cheerfully, casting a cozy glow into the room. Ahead and slightly to the right was a scarred wooden bar with the standard liquor bottles and glasses clustered on shelves behind it. The ceiling was low, heavy beams dark with age, and the floor flagstone, worn smooth by hundreds of feet. Around the room clustered comfy chairs, perfect for relaxing with a drink. There were small groupings of proper tables and chairs for more easily eating whatever heavenly smelling delicacy was currently cooking in the kitchen. According to the chalkboard, the daily specials were fish and chips and sausage and mash.

The pub was small, but chock full of ambience. A man who looked about a hundred perched on a stool, his newsboy cap pulled low over his forehead. He hunched over his half-empty pint of beer. Two couples were gathered near the window—not that they could see much in this storm—sharing a meal and talking in low voices. Otherwise the place was empty. No one looked up when we entered which I found very odd.

"Why don't we sit near the fire," Lucas suggested. "Warm ourselves up."

I shrugged. "Sure. I could dry out."

I sank into one of the twin leather chairs next to the fire. On the small occasional table between them was a menu. The cover carried the name of the pub: Beast and Bauble. They did love their wacky names around here.

"Anything to drink?" Lucas asked as he draped his jacket over the back of the other chair.

"Blackberry bourbon, of course."

He smiled. "Of course. But I've a feeling they might not have it."

I sighed. "Fine. Baileys and coffee. Heavy on the Baileys." I might be driving, but I wasn't going anywhere at the moment and neither was the car.

Lucas collected our drinks from the bartender and settled in. "This is perfect." A dreamy smile curved his full lips.

I eyed him narrowly. "What's perfect?"

"This village. This pub. Don't you feel it? The atmosphere?"

Usually I was the one waxing poetic about things. This turn of events made me uneasy. "You want to research *this* village for your novel?"

"Why not?" He took a sip of his drink.

"We haven't even seen the place. It might be awful."

He grinned, gray eyes twinkling. "Oh, I've a good feeling."

"Great," I muttered around my coffee. "Now he's getting feelings."

Lucas merely chuckled.

The old man turned on his stool and eyeballed us mournfully. "Don't get many visitors," he said. "Welcome to Chipping Poggs." He raised his half-empty pint glass and then slugged back a good swallow.

"Thanks," Lucas and I chimed before taking more genteel sips of our own drinks.

Chipping Poggs? What a name. I exchanged a glance with Lucas who looked more excited than ever.

"Told you so," he muttered.

"Simon Briggs. What brings you folks this way?" the old man asked, wiping his mouth on his sleeve. I noticed thickets of white hair sprouting out his ears and down his nostrils and wondered vaguely if he had any left on his head.

"I'm Viola Roberts and this is my boyfriend, Lucas Salvatore," I said. "Is there a petrol station in town?" I wasn't about to admit we were searching for a village with "atmosphere" for my boyfriend's next book.

"'Fraid not. Closest one be about half-way between here and Chipping Camden."

"We're a bit lost," Lucas admitted. "We were trying to get back to Oxford for the night, but we must've taken a wrong turn somewhere."

"Oh, aye, that you did. But not to worry. We've got a lovely inn here in town."

"I didn't see one on the way in," I said. Granted, it had been pouring down rain so I couldn't see much of anything, but there definitely hadn't been anything that appeared inn-like.

"You wouldn't," Simon said. "It's on the other side of town." He waved vaguely. "Up at the old manor house. The family couldn't afford the upkeep, so they turned it into an inn. Very popular with tourists and whatnot. And at least it's not as haunted as the church." He waggled his bushy eyebrows, clearly hoping to pique our interest. He did not hope in vain.

"You have a haunted church? Is that even possible?" I asked.

"Oh, aye." His eyes twinkled, obviously realizing he had a captive audience. "Let me tell you about the ghosts of Chipping Poggs."

The Remains in the Rectory is now available at most online retailers

Shéa MacLeod

A Note from Shéa

Thank you for reading. If you enjoyed this book, I'd appreciate it if you'd help others find it so they can enjoy it too.

- Lend it: This e-book is lending-enabled, so feel free to share it with your friends, readers' groups, and discussion boards.

- Review it: Let other potential readers know what you liked or didn't like about the story.

Book updates can be found at www.sheamacleod.com

Shéa MacLeod

About Shéa MacLeod

Shéa MacLeod is the author of the bestselling paranormal series, Sunwalker Saga, as well as the award nominated cozy mystery series Viola Roberts Cozy Mysteries. She has dreamed of writing novels since before she could hold a crayon. She totally blames her mother.

She resides in the leafy green hills outside Portland, Oregon where she indulges in her fondness for strong coffee, Ancient Aliens reruns, lemon curd, and dragons. She can usually be found at her desk dreaming of ways to kill people (or vampires). Fictionally speaking, of course.

Shéa MacLeod

Other Books by Shea Shéa MacLeod

54255700R00064

Made in the USA
Columbia, SC
27 March 2019